Brownies

With thanks to Helen Channa, Susan Cole, Nithya Rae and Hannah Redford at Girlguiding UK for all their help and advice

STRIPES PUBLISHING
An imprint of Magi Publications
1 The Coda Centre, 189 Munster Road,
London SW6 6AW

A paperback original. First published in Great Britain in 2009
Published by arrangement with Girlguiding UK.
Brownie logo, uniforms and badges copyright © Girlguiding UK
Text copyright © Caroline Plaisted, 2009. Illustrations copyright © Katie Wood, 2009

ISBN: 978-1-84715-102-5

A CIP catalogue record for this book is available
from the British Library.

Printed and bound in the UK.
2 4 6 8 10 9 7 5 3

Meet the Brownies

Katie

Katie, Grace's twin, is super sporty and likes to play games and win. She wants to get every Brownie badge and her Six is Foxes!

Jamila

Jamila's got too many brothers, so she loves Brownies because NO BOYS ARE ALLOWED! Jamila is a Badger!

Ellie

Awesome at art and crafts, Ellie used to be a Rainbow and likes making new friends. Ellie is a Hedgehog!

Charlie

Animal-crazy Charlie has a guinea pig called Nibbles. She loves Brownie quizzes and Pow Wows. Her Six is Squirrels!

Grace

Grace is Katie's twin sister and she's ballet bonkers. Grace enjoys going on Brownie outings, and she is a Rabbit!

I am rabbit

Chapter 1

It was Tuesday evening, the start of another
meeting of the 1st Badenbridge
Brownies, and all the girls were
singing at the tops of their voices.
Vicky and Sam, the Brownie
Leaders, were holding up their hands,
linked in an arch that the Brownies were
skipping under, smiling as they sang.

At the end of the song, the
Brownies formed the Brownie
Ring, as they always did when the
Sixes got together at the beginning
of each meeting. The Sixes were
the groups that made up the Brownie unit.

The 1st Badenbridge Brownies' Sixes were
Badgers, Foxes, Squirrels, Rabbits and
Hedgehogs.

As the last Brownie joined the Ring,
all the girls put up their right hands and
fell silent.

"Welcome!" Vicky smiled. "It's really
good to see you all. Why don't you sit down
and we'll tell you what we'll be doing this
evening."

Jamila, one of the Badgers, smiled across
the circle at her four best friends. They were
Charlie, who was a Squirrel, Grace, a Rabbit,
Ellie, one of the Hedgehogs, and Katie, who
was a Fox. The five girls had only recently
been enrolled as Brownies and loved getting
involved with all the fun activities.

"In just under four weeks' time it is going
to be a very important day for Brownies

across the world," Sam said.

All around the Ring, the Brownies sat up excitedly, wondering what she was going to tell them.

"Because," Sam continued, "the twenty-second of February is World Thinking Day. Would any of you newer Brownies like to have a guess at why it's called Thinking Day?"

Katie's hand shot up.

"Please, Sam!" she said, waving her hand eagerly.

"Yes, Katie?" Sam smiled.

"Is it called Thinking Day because it's the day we all have to think?" Katie suggested.

"Well, sort of," said Sam. "But can anyone tell me what we especially have to think about on Thinking Day that we don't think about on other days? Brownies who've been with us for a while – can any of you remember?"

This time, lots of hands shot up.

Sam smiled. "Izzy, what do you remember?"

Izzy was the Sixer of the Badgers.

"Isn't it something to do with Brownies in other countries?"

"It is!" said Sam. "And can anyone remember whose birthdays Thinking Day celebrates? How about you, Boo?"

Boo was Charlie's big sister and she'd been a Brownie for a couple of years. She was also the Seconder for the Rabbits.

"Oh!" Boo said, shooting up her hand and forgetting that Sam had already asked her.

Sam laughed. "Go on then, Boo."

"The twenty-second of February is the day that Lord and Lady Baden-Powell were born!" said Boo.

"That's right!" Sam replied. "Lord Baden-Powell started Boy Scouts and Girl Guides in the last century, and Lady Baden-Powell played an important role in Guides for many years. Can you imagine, girls? The first Brownies were around a hundred years ago!"

The Brownies gasped.

Sam smiled at them. "Every year, on the twenty-second of February, Brownies all over the world remember Lord and Lady Baden-Powell. They also remember other Brownies around the world."

"So," said Vicky, taking out a book, "to get us thinking about Thinking Day, I thought I would read you a story so that we can all learn a bit more about how the Brownies started…"

Vicky told the 1st Badenbridge Brownies all about how the Scouts and Cubs started, but only for boys, a long time ago in 1907. She explained that one day, Lord Baden-Powell arranged a huge meeting for the Scouts. Some girls turned up because they wanted to be Scouts too, and they refused to leave when they were told it was only for boys. They formed their own girls-only unit and Lord Baden-Powell was so impressed that he asked his sister, Agnes Baden-Powell, to help start girl guiding around the world.

When Vicky had finished reading the story, Grace immediately put up her hand.

"Vicky?" she asked. "Katie and I, we've got a cousin in Australia and she's a Brownie.

Which other countries are there Brownies in?"

"Well," said Vicky, "there are Brownies all over the UK, and in a hundred and forty-four other countries around the world as well! Thinking Day is a chance to think about everyone in the guiding family."

"How many Brownies are there around the world then?" Megan, the Sixer of the Squirrels, wanted to know.

"There are about ten million Rainbows, Brownies, Guides and Senior Section members in total. Imagine that!" said Vicky. "But not all Brownies are called Brownies. In some countries they have different names. And in other countries *all* the girls, however old they are, are called Guides.

"Wow!" the Brownies said in surprise.

"So," said Sam. "Thinking Day. We're lucky because we have been given permission to hold our Thinking Day celebration on the High Street this year. We'll let you know more about that soon."

The Brownies exchanged excited glances – a celebration on the High Street!

"But now," Sam continued, "as part of our Thinking Day preparations, we've got some colouring sheets for you to do, which are packed with facts about Brownies around the world," said Sam.

"So if the Sixers could come up and collect the sheets," said Vicky, "perhaps the Seconders could get out the colouring boxes, ready for you to begin. Over to your Six tables, Brownies!"

The Brownies all stood up and rushed off. They couldn't wait to find out more!

Chapter 2

The Six tables were buzzing with activity. As soon as the Sixers handed out the colouring sheets, the Brownies got to work.

"Wow!" exclaimed Ellie as she read one of the facts on the sheet. "It says here that if all the Brownies in the UK held hands, they would make a chain eight hundred and fifty kilometres long!"

"That's amazing!" her Sixer, Lauren, replied. "Who's got a red colouring pen? Can I use it, please?"

"So how many Brownies make eight hundred and fifty kilometres?" Amy the Seconder wanted to know.

"Five hundred thousand!" said Poppy, another one of the Hedgehogs. "Loads!"

Over on the Badgers' table, Izzy the Sixer and Holly the Seconder were helping the other Brownies with their sheets.

"It says here," said Chloe, "that there are Brownies in twenty-five countries in Europe!"

"And Europe's just one of the areas of the world that has Brownies," said Jamila.

"Yeah, it says there are Brownies in five regions: the Arab region, Africa, Asia Pacific, Europe and the Western Hemisphere," Jasmine pointed out. "They're on this map – look!"

"I didn't know there were so many places with Brownies and Guides," Jamila admitted.

"Do you think they all wear the same outfit as we do?" Holly wondered.

"Do you think they all do the same things as we do?" Jasmine asked.

"And do you think they are all thinking about Brownies round the world tonight, just like we are?" Lauren said.

"Course they are!" said Daisy, who had come over to the Badgers table to see how they were getting on. Daisy was a Guide, but she came to Brownies to help out as a Young Leader. "Come on," she said. "Let's see if we

18

can finish these sheets before Vicky and Sam start our Pow Wow."

A Pow Wow was a special meeting when the Brownies got together to discuss the things they'd like to do at Brownies. Everyone was equal at a Pow Wow and all the Brownies got the chance to speak and say what they thought.

On all the Six tables, Brownies were busily colouring and reading their sheets. When everyone had finished, Sam and Vicky called all the girls over to the middle of the hall, then everyone sat down in the Brownie Ring.

"OK, Brownies," said Vicky. "I thought we should have a Pow Wow to talk a bit more about Thinking Day."

"Yes," said Sam. "We were wondering if any of you had ideas for things we might do

to pass on Brownie smiles and our Brownie Promise to help other Brownies."

"We could go on an outing with the First Powelton Brownies," suggested Charlie. "They're not far away."

"Good idea!" Vicky smiled. "But we do already go with them to the Christmas pantomime each year. I was wondering more about Brownies in another country…"

"Yes," said Sam. "We were thinking that we could perhaps choose one country or region and find out about the Brownies there."

"How about Africa?" suggested Katie. "There was a thing about children in Africa on *Newsround* the other day."

There was a murmur of recognition from lots of the other Brownies who had seen the same television programme.

"There are lots of Brownies in Africa," said Vicky. "That's a good thought."

"How big a country is Africa?" asked Ashvini.

"It isn't a country," said Jessica, the Sixer of the Foxes, who was the oldest Brownie in the unit. "It's a continent. The African continent is made up of lots of different countries. We did a project about it at school."

"My auntie works in Africa," said Sukia, who was waving her hand excitedly in the air. She was a Hedgehog, and was sitting next to Ellie in the Ring.

"Does she?" asked Vicky. "What job does she do there?"

"She's a doctor," said Sukia. "She works for a charity called HealthHelp. In a country called Senegal."

"What does HealthHelp do?" asked Emma, the Seconder of the Foxes.

"They make sure people have injections and medical care. You know, so that they don't get sick. I can ask my mum about it if you like," Sukia said.

"That's a great idea," said Vicky. "Please do."

"So," said Sam, looking round the Ring, "would you all like to find out a bit more about Brownies in Africa?"

"Yes!" cried all the girls at once.

"Great," said Sam. "Why don't you all do some more thinking before next week? Then you can come back to our next meeting with some ideas of what we can do!"

"OK, Pow Wow over," said Vicky. "Who'd like to make a Brownie friendship bracelet?"

"Me!" yelled every Brownie in the room.

"Come on then!" Sam giggled. "Choose your favourite colours from all these threads we've got, then we'll show you how to make your bracelet!"

After making some really pretty bracelets, the girls played a version of "It" called Chain Gang, where every Brownie caught by "It" had to hold hands and form a chain to catch the next one. Before they knew it, the Brownie meeting was nearly over.

"Now," said Vicky, as the Brownies gathered together again in the Ring. "It's time for our Thought for the Week. Jasmine has written this week's thought, and she is going to read it for us."

Jasmine stood up, clutching the book the Brownies wrote their Thoughts for the Week in. A different Brownie did it every week. She turned to the right page and began.

"We think about all the fun we have at Brownies and all the friends we have made here. We will think about them during the week and smile at them when we see them. We think about Vicky and Sam. Oh – and we'll smile at them and any other grown-ups we see during the week, too!"

At school a couple of days later, Jamila, Grace, Katie, Ellie and Charlie were sitting on their favourite bench in the playground, talking about Thinking Day.

"Do you think the Brownies in Africa have a hall like ours to meet in?" wondered Grace.

"I expect some of them do," said Jamila. "But I'm sure there will be others who don't have such a nice place."

"Yes," said Ellie. "Some children aren't as lucky as us. So maybe there are some Brownies who aren't as lucky as us either."

"You know that Sukia was talking about her auntie?" said Katie. "You know – the one who's a doctor?"

Her four best friends nodded.

"Well, perhaps we could do something to help the children and Brownies who go to

the clinic where she works," suggested Katie.

"You mean raise some money for them?" wondered Jamila. "Like when they do appeals on the telly?"

"Exactly!" said Katie.

"That's a brilliant idea!" exclaimed Ellie. "I think we should tell Vicky about it next week."

Chapter 3

On Friday morning, as Charlie and Ellie arrived at school, they saw Mrs Sadler, their head teacher, struggling to open a door because her arms were full of books. As they tried hard to be good Brownies, even when they weren't in their Brownie outfits, they rushed over to lend a hand.

"We'll help you, Miss," said Ellie, holding open the door.

"Yes – I'll carry some books," said Charlie, taking some of the ones that were wobbling on the top of the pile.

"Thank you, girls!" smiled Mrs Sadler. "That's really helpful and thoughtful."

"You're welcome," grinned Charlie.
"Brownies do a good turn every day."

"I remember," said the head teacher.
"I used to be a Brownie when I was your
age. Only I don't think I did quite as many
good turns as you girls seem to do! I must
remember to tell Vicky what good Brownies
you are. Vicky used to come to school here
as well, you know!"

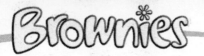

"Wow!" the girls said, grinning. They couldn't wait to tell the others that Vicky had been at their school and raced across the playground to find them.

"Cool!" exclaimed Jamila, after Charlie had filled them in. "How brilliant is that!"

"I wonder if Sam came here too?" wondered Katie.

"What do you think they looked like when they were at school," asked Grace.

"And what do you reckon they wore at Brownies?" said Ellie. "Do you think they had Brownie clothes like ours?"

"I've seen a photo of my mum when she was a Brownie," commented Charlie. "She had to wear a brown dress and a funny yellow tie thingy round her neck – it looked really weird!"

"Let's ask Vicky and Sam if they've got photos of themselves too!" suggested Jamila.

"We can do it next week at Brownies!" Grace giggled.

After school on Monday, the five best friends were playing together at Charlie's house.

"Why don't we come up with some ways we can raise money for Thinking Day," Katie said.

"Good idea," said Charlie.

"We could bake cakes and sell them," suggested Jamila, who always seemed to be hungry.

"Yum!" agreed Charlie.

"We could be sponsored for something!" Katie exclaimed. "For running or swimming."

"Or maybe for being silent," said Grace, who didn't fancy doing something as energetic as a race.

"Or we could make other things besides cakes," suggested Ellie. "And sell those too."

"What sort of things?" asked Katie.

"Hmmm…" sighed Ellie. "Maybe some crafts?"

The others thought that sounded cool.

"Well, let's talk to Vicky and Sam about it tomorrow," suggested Jamila. "Come on – we've got to learn our spellings for school. Then we can open the packet of biscuits I brought with me!"

Jamila, Grace, Ellie, Katie and Charlie were back at Brownies again the following night.

"Please, Vicky!" said Katie as soon as she arrived in the hall. "We've thought of loads of things to do for Thinking Day!"

"Excellent!" Vicky grinned. "Lots of other Brownies have got exciting ideas too. I can't wait to hear them all."

Katie hadn't thought that Vicky would say that. She hoped that no one else had the same ideas as she and her friends had.

"Looks like we need another Pow Wow," suggested Sam.

Vicky nodded.

"All girls into the Brownie Ring as quick as you can!" Vicky announced. "Then we can have our Pow Wow."

The hall had been filled with excited chatter as the girls greeted each other and

gathered in their Sixes. But as soon as Vicky
called them, they raced to sit down in the
Brownie Ring.

"Now," said Sam. "It's great that you all
did so much thinking about Thinking Day!
So, I've got a very long piece of paper and a
pen with lots of ink in it, ready to write
down all your ideas."

"Who's got the first suggestion then?"
asked Vicky.

Caitlin put up her hand.

"You know you were talking about the
Brownies in Africa?" she said. "Well, I
thought we could find out a bit more about
them. Like how many Brownies there are,
and in which African countries?"

"Good idea," said Sam, writing it down.

There was a murmur of approval from the
other Brownies.

Then it was Lottie, one of the Foxes, who got to speak.

"I thought we could make a Thinking Day cake," she said. "We could write the names of all the countries in the world that have Brownies on it."

All the Brownies thought that sounded like a delicious idea.

Katie shot up her hand. "Please!" she said, holding her hand as high as she could.

"You *are* keen to share your idea," said Vicky, smiling. "Go ahead, Katie."

"I thought … we thought … that's Grace, Ellie, Jamila, Charlie and me," she explained. "We thought we should maybe do something for Sukia's auntie's health clinic. Maybe raise some money to help them."

Before Vicky could answer, Sukia's hand shot up too.

"Please, Vicky and Sam!" said Sukia. "Mum and I sent my auntie an email and asked her about HealthHelp."

"Oh wonderful," said Sam. "What can you tell us about it?"

"Auntie says they run clinics for mums and babies, and they also care for older people as well," said Sukia. "They rely on donations to pay for the clinics and doctors."

Katie put up her hand again, but didn't wait for Vicky to say she could speak before she said, "So we *do* need to help them! We thought we could make things and sell them."

"Hmm… What sort of things, do you think?" Sam wondered.

"Arts and crafts" suggested Ellie, "such as cards and gift tags."

"And painted flower pots," added Charlie.

"How about sewing some lavender bags?" said Grace.

Lots of other Brownies had great ideas for things like bookmarks, badges, coasters – all sorts!

"I think we have an excellent list of ideas for Thinking Day," said Sam.

"And I think I have another one," Vicky stated. "Remember we're celebrating Thinking Day on a Saturday? Perhaps, as part of our celebration on the High Street, we could hold a Craft Sale to raise our funds for HealthHelp on that day!"

"Yes!" the Brownies all agreed at once.

"And if lots of Brownies are making things," Sam pointed out, "then perhaps some of you

could make things that would link in with
your Craft badge. If you'd like to."

There was a buzz of interest.

"What do you have to do for
your Craft badge?" Ellie asked.

"Oh, I've done it!" said
Holly. "I had to make three
things – there's stuff about it in the
Brownie Badge Book."

"Let's do it!" exclaimed Katie, who was
keen to get as many badges as possible.

"Some of you have still got the
Wildlife explorer and Out
and about badges to
finish," Sam pointed
out. "But there's nothing
to stop you starting another one."

"Great!" all the Brownies said.

"Now, has anyone got any more ideas

or questions before we move on to something else?" Vicky asked.

Ellie's hand shot up.

"Oh please, Vicky!"

"Yes, Ellie?" Vicky smiled.

"Our head teacher, Mrs Sadler, told us that you used to be a Brownie when you were our age!"

There was a gasp of astonishment around the room.

Vicky and Sam laughed.

"We both used to be Brownies," said Vicky.

"We were both with First Badenbridge Brownies at the same time," added Sam.

There was another gasp from the Brownies.

"Have you got photos?" Charlie asked.

"Do you know," said Sam, "I think we have."

"Can we see them?" most of the Brownies around the room said at the same time.

"Let me see if I can find one," said Vicky, smiling.

"Come on," said Sam, looking at her watch. "We'd better get on with our Thinking Day plans!"

Chapter 4

By the end of the Pow Wow, the Brownies had decided to come back to their next meeting with as much craft material as they could. They planned to collect bits of coloured paper, ribbons, scraps of fabrics, stickers, buttons, beads – all sorts!

Sam had also suggested that each girl should find out something more about Senegal and come to next week's meeting with an exciting fact. So, after school the next day, the five best friends met up with Jamila and Charlie's mums and paid a visit to the library. Charlie's sisters, Boo and baby Georgia, had come along with them.

41

"Here's a book about Africa," said Jamila. "Let's see what it says."

The five friends thumbed through the book, looking for the section on Senegal.

"There!" Katie pointed out.

"I can't see," said Ellie, who was at the back of the group. "Can you read it out, Jamila?"

"Sure," she replied. "It says the capital city is Dakar."

"One of us should write this stuff down," suggested Charlie, "so that we can take it back to Brownies."

"Good idea," said Boo. "Well done, sis!"

"Katie should do it," said Ellie. "She's got the best handwriting."

Katie blushed at the praise. "OK," she said. She rummaged in her school bag, found a notebook and pen and began to write.

"Senegal's official language is French. How weird is that? Speaking French in Africa!" added Charlie. "But most of the people also speak something called … Wo … Wo … Wolo … Oh! How do you think that sounds?" she asked, writing down the word "Wolof".

"Let's see," said Grace. "Urmm … how about Wol-off?"

"Wol-off. OK," Katie replied.

"There are eleven regions in Senegal and eleven million people live there," said Jamila.

"And the main religion is Islam," added Grace.

"Do you think there are many Brownies there?" wondered Ellie, thinking about Caitlin's idea.

"How can we find out?" asked Katie.

"There's stuff about Brownies in Africa and other countries in my *Brownies Adventure On*

book," said Boo. As Boo had been
a Brownie for a couple of years
already, she had a different
Brownie book to the ones that
the younger Brownies had for
projects and ideas. "You can see it
if you want," Boo added. "But it's
at home at the moment, of course."

"Please!" said Jamila and Grace.

After walking back to Charlie's house, the
five Brownie friends and Boo raced upstairs
to Boo and Charlie's bedroom.

"Here," said Boo, taking out her copy of
Brownies Adventure On from her Brownie
Promise Box.

"Thanks," said Jamila, flicking through
the book.

"It's somewhere near the back," Boo mentioned helpfully. "There's stuff about crafts from around the world too."

"There it is!" declared Katie.

Jamila and Katie looked closely at the page.

"There's lots about making African necklaces here," said Katie.

"Oooh!" said art-loving Ellie. "Maybe we could make some for the Craft Sale! What do you think?"

"That's a really cool idea," agreed Jamila. "What else does it say?"

"Look, it says here that there's a website about Guides around the world!" said Charlie.

"Let's go and surf it!" said Grace.

"I'll go and ask Mum if it's OK first," said Boo, and everyone followed her downstairs.

A few minutes later, they were on the WAGGGS website. WAGGGS stood for the World Association of Girl Guides and Girl Scouts. Their website had lots of information about Brownies and Guides all around the world.

"Let's see if we can find Senegal," Boo suggested, typing the word into the search box. "There!"

"More than two thousand girls are Brownies and Guides in Senegal!" Grace declared, as she read what it said on the screen.

"I'll write that down," said Katie, adding it to the list they had started in the library.

"I can't wait to tell Vicky and Sam what we've found out!" Jamila grinned.

"Or to tell them about making African crafts for the Sale," added Ellie.

"Come on," said Charlie. "Let's go and see if tea is ready!"

"I'm starving!" said Jamila.

"Me too!" agreed the others, as they raced into the kitchen.

On Saturday, Katie and Grace were in the supermarket with their dad when a friendly face greeted them by the shelves stacked with breakfast cereals.

"Hello, Brownies!" Vicky grinned.

"Hi, Vicky!" said Grace.

"Oh – it's just brilliant that we've seen you! We've got loads of things to tell you!" Katie spluttered.

"Well, that's nice!" said Vicky.

"It's about Senegal and Brownies," said Katie. "We—"

But before Katie could say any more, Grace interrupted her.

"Perhaps we should wait until the next meeting so that the others can tell you about it too," suggested Grace. "Because we've all been working on the ideas together. With Boo too."

"Good idea," Vicky agreed.

"But I've just got to tell you Ellie's idea to make African crafts!" And before her twin could stop her, Katie explained about the African beads and necklaces that they'd seen in Boo's Brownie book.

"Well," said Vicky with a thoughtful look on her face. "What a good idea! An African-themed Craft Sale. Do you know, I think that's given me an idea as well."

"What's that?" asked Grace and Katie.

"Now *that*," said Vicky, "would be telling…"

Chapter 5

Grace worried all weekend.

"Why didn't you wait to tell Vicky with the others, like I said?" she asked Katie.

"What's the big deal?" replied her sister. "After all, Vicky thought it was a good idea, didn't she? And she's going to do more about it before Brownies on Tuesday. Honestly! I don't know what you're going on about."

But Grace wasn't so sure. She even tried to talk to Jamila about it at school, to see if she thought the others would be angry. But they were all so busy there was never a moment to catch Jamila on her own.

On Tuesday night, Vicky and Sam called all the Brownies into the Ring. The two Leaders grinned at a lady who was sitting next to them.

"Girls," said Vicky, "I'd like to introduce you to Eugenia. She's a friend of mine and she's come to join us tonight to help us with our Craft Sale."

"Hello," Eugenia smiled at everyone.

"Hello!" all the Brownies called back.

"Shall we give Eugenia a Brownie welcome?" Sam suggested.

The Brownies enthusiastically agreed. Brownie welcomes were special – they all said "Welcome" three times as they clapped their hands first above their heads, then to their left, and to their right.

"Thank you," said Eugenia. "That was lovely."

Jamila, Charlie, Grace, Ellie and Katie smiled at each other, wondering what sorts of things they were going to make with Eugenia.

"We're looking forward to hearing your facts about Senegal later, but first, we've had some good news about Thinking Day," said Vicky. "The supermarket on the High Street has kindly agreed to let us set up our stall of goodies right outside their main window!"

"Yeah!" the Brownies exclaimed.

"Now I know that all of you have brought in things that we can use for making our crafts tonight," said Vicky. "And lots of you have already started making things, which is great – really great."

All the Brownies smiled at their Leader.

"I'm sure you're all bursting with ideas,"

Vicky continued. "In fact, the other day I bumped into two of our newest Brownies, Katie and Grace, and Katie told me about a brilliant idea they'd had for our crafts."

Ellie, Jamila and Charlie looked at the twins in surprise. They hadn't known that Katie and Grace had told Vicky about Ellie's idea, but they were pleased that Vicky thought it was so good.

"Katie suggested to me that we should make some special African crafts to sell on Thinking Day," Vicky said. "I thought that was an excellent idea. What do you think?"

All the Brownies, except for four of them, agreed wholeheartedly. Jamila and Charlie looked puzzled, and Grace looked anxious, but Ellie looked furious. They all knew that the idea hadn't been Katie's. It was *Ellie's* brilliant idea! *She* was the one who'd

thought of it! And now Katie was sitting there grinning because all the other Brownies thought it was *her* idea!

"So," said Vicky, "Eugenia is going to help us make some African crafts tonight. But before we go off into our

Sixes to get started, Eugenia is going to tell us a little more about herself."

Ellie glowered at Katie across the Brownie Ring. How could Katie be so sneaky?

But she didn't have time to brood on it any longer because Eugenia stood up to speak.

"It's lovely to be back at Brownies," said Eugenia. "I used to be a Brownie in South Africa a long time ago. After I left school, I became a teacher and then, a year ago, I got the chance to come to the UK to do an exchange at a school. I'm going back to South Africa next year."

The Brownies sat up straight and listened, fascinated, as Eugenia told them all about the things she got up to as a Brownie and then a Guide. She explained what her guiding outfit had looked like and the sort of things that Brownies and Guides do now in the African region.

"Brownies are all over Africa," said Eugenia. "Some of the girls in my school are Brownies and they are all little girls just like you! They all make the same Promise that you have made: they do their best, they lend

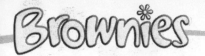

a hand, love their God, and they serve their country!"

"Wow!" said the Brownies in the Ring.

"Now," Eugenia smiled, "let's get making some beads!"

Ellie wanted to say something to Katie, but the Brownies all had to go into their Sixes to get started on their crafts. Ellie couldn't believe Katie hadn't tried to correct Vicky when she'd praised her for an idea that wasn't hers. And what was worse, Katie hadn't even noticed that she was mad!

At their Six tables, using flour, kitchen roll and water, the Brownies were busily making beads under the guidance of Daisy, Vicky, Eugenia and Sam. Eugenia and the Brownie Leaders went round the Six tables explaining

what to do. Soon all the girls were shaping blobs of damp paper around straws.

"This is brilliant!" Jamila declared to Eugenia. "The straw leaves the hole in the bead so that we can thread it!"

"Cool!" said Izzy, who was Jamila's Sixer. "I can't wait for them to dry so that we can paint them!"

All around the room, Brownies chatted and laughed as they worked. They each made enough beads to make either a necklace or a bracelet.

"OK, Brownies," declared Sam, putting up her right hand.

Instantly, every one else did the same and fell silent. Even Eugenia did it – just like the Brownies and Guides in South Africa!

"The beads need to dry now," said Sam. "So leave them on your Six tables, go and wash your hands, and come over to have a drink. Then we're going to learn some African songs with Eugenia!"

"I can't believe that you told Vicky the African idea was yours!" Charlie said to Katie as they washed their hands.

"I didn't!" she replied.

"You so did!" said Ellie. "And it wasn't

yours – it was mine!"

"I'm sorry Vicky got it wrong," Katie said,
"but does it really matter now?"

Ellie glared at her.

Jamila gave her friend a hug. "It would have been nice if we could *all* have told her about Ellie's idea."

"Well, if we'd waited for tonight to tell Vicky, then we wouldn't be having fun with Eugenia now, would we?" Katie pointed out.

It was true.

"And Katie did tell Vicky that it was Ellie's idea when we bumped into her last week," Grace explained. "She must have forgotten…"

"It still doesn't explain why Katie didn't correct Vicky tonight!" Ellie snapped, leaving the washroom to return to the hall.

"Are you all good at singing?" Eugenia asked as all the Brownies gathered together in the hall.

"Yes!" the Brownies called out.

"Are you all good at learning actions?" Eugenia asked.

"Yes!" the Brownies called out again.

"Then I'm going to teach you a song and dance that we do at my school in South Africa!" declared Eugenia. "It's called Impuka Nekati – that means Mice and Cats – and it's from a part of the country called Zululand. I need the mice on this side and the cats over there!"

Groups of Brownies raced off in opposite directions, ready for more fun.

Chapter 6

Ellie left Brownies so quickly that night, that the others didn't get a chance to speak to her. Next day at school, Ellie went straight over to Bethany, one of the Squirrels from Brownies, to play with her and her friends, completely ignoring Katie, Charlie, Jamila and Grace.

"Ellie!" called Grace. "Ellie – over here! Hey – Ellie!"

Ellie didn't take any notice.

"She's still cross about last night," said Charlie.

"I know," said Grace. "I feel really bad about it."

"What – Brownies?" Katie said. "Is Ellie still cross about that?"

"Oh, Katie!" exclaimed Jamila.

"Listen," said Katie. "I told Vicky that Ellie'd had the idea when we saw her in the supermarket," explained Katie.

"We know that, but at Brownies Vicky told everyone it was your idea," said Jamila, "and you didn't correct her, did you? So everyone thought you had come up with it."

Katie felt her cheeks go pink. "Oh," she said. "I see what you mean … but I didn't tell a fib or anything! I didn't mean to make her think it was only mine."

"Maybe not," said Jamila, "but we've got to make Ellie realize that. I'm going over to speak to her."

Charlie followed her over.

"Hi, Ellie." Jamila smiled. "You OK?"

Ellie didn't answer.

"Hey Jamila, hey Charlie," said Bethany. "Have you come over to play with us?"

"Sure," replied Jamila, joining in their skipping game with Charlie.

They played for a few minutes and then the bell rang. It was time to line up ready to go into the classroom.

Jamila and Charlie made sure they stood behind Ellie.

"We know why you aren't talking to us," said Charlie.

"It's not you I'm not talking to," Ellie whispered. "It's Katie – how could she be so mean?"

"I don't think she did it on purpose," explained Jamila.

"Yeah, right," said Ellie crossly. "She always wants people to think everything is her idea!"

"Oh Ellie, I'm sure that's not true," said Charlie. "She just didn't have a chance to explain to Vicky, that's all."

"What – like all evening she didn't?" hissed Ellie.

But her friends couldn't reply because it was time for their first lesson of the day.

At lunchtime, Grace and the others told
Katie that it was time she made up with Ellie.
It wasn't until after they'd eaten their lunch
and were allowed out into the playground
again that they got the chance to catch Ellie
on her own.

"Oh, Ellie," sighed Katie. "I'm really sorry
– I shouldn't have said anything to Vicky
about the African crafts until Brownies last
night. But I promise, I really did tell her it
was your idea!"

Ellie looked at her, but didn't say anything. She'd been missing her friends all day, but she wanted Katie to realize how she felt.

"It's true," said Grace. "Katie really did tell Vicky, only she must have got confused."

"I promise I'll never do anything like that again," said Katie. "I'll always wait to share things in future. Honest!"

"Can we all be friends again, Ellie?" Jamila asked.

"We're really missing you," said Charlie.

"We're totally miserable without you!"
declared Grace.

"Please be my friend," Katie pleaded.

Ellie looked at them all and smiled.

"Friends then!"

"Yesss!" the others replied.

"Come on," said Jamila. "Let's see if we
can remember that song that Eugenia taught
us last night!"

That evening, the five Brownie best friends
met up at Ellie's house to make crafts. They
made more beads and painted them in the
bright, bold colours that Eugenia had
suggested. They also made more friendship
bracelets from long strands of yarn, and some
beanbags in the shape of giant frogs, like ones
that they'd made once at school. When the

painted beads were dry, the girls threaded them to make necklaces and bracelets.

"These look cool!" Ellie declared, holding one of the necklaces up.

"I think the frogs do too," agreed Katie. "And it's brilliant that they'll go towards our Craft badge as well!"

"Yes, they will!" Ellie grinned.

"Hey, I've put all the material and stuff that we've collected into a big shopping bag my mum gave me," Charlie said.

"Brilliant," said Jamila, yawning.

Just then, her mum arrived. She was going to give Charlie and Ellie a lift too.

Jamila's mum grinned. "Come on, girls – time to go home. I'm sure all your parents will be keen for you to be in bed!"

On Thursday night, the five girls met up to do some more work on their Wildlife explorer badges. They had very nearly finished a project about trees that they'd been working on together. It was one of the last tasks they had to do before they actually completed their badge. It was going to be the first Brownie badge that any of them had completed and they were all really excited about it.

On Friday night, there was a netball match at school. Katie and Charlie were playing in the team and Jamila, Grace and Ellie stayed to cheer them on. The score was level right up until the last few minutes of the game, so it was extra exciting when Badenbridge Primary School won!

But on Saturday, after Jamila had been to her music group, and Grace had finished her ballet class, the girls all met up for a final and massive craft session at Jamila's house. They made more beads and painted them. They also painted some flowerpots in the same bright colours as the beads.

"I think these are my favourite!" Katie declared, holding up one of them when it was dry.

"I hope that Vicky and Sam like them," said Grace.

"Course they will!" Charlie grinned as she packed everything into the big bag.

During the week, the friends had been
asking everyone they could think of if they
had any old scraps of fabric, or braid, or
ribbons – anything they could use for making
crafts at Brownies. They'd also been asking
people for any other bits and pieces that they
could sell at the sale to raise funds for
HealthHelp.

"You'll need to make sure you take the
bag to Brownies," warned Katie.

"I know," Charlie replied. "I won't forget!"

On Tuesday morning, in the playground at
school, Charlie raced over to Ellie first thing.

"Oh, Ellie!" she said, tears welling up in
her eyes.

"What's up?" Ellie looked at her friend,
concerned. "What's happened?"

"It's the bag," explained Charlie tearfully.
"The one with all the Brownie craft stuff in.
I've lost it!"

Chapter 7

"You can't have lost it!" said Ellie.

"I put the bag at the end of my bed so I wouldn't forget it. And then I went to get it this morning, ready for Brownies tonight, and couldn't find it!" sighed Charlie, wiping away the tears from her eyes. "What am I going to do?" she whispered. "The others are going to be mad with me!"

"Are you sure you looked in the right place?" Ellie asked quietly.

"Course I am!" sobbed Charlie. "I'm sorry. I just don't know what to do!"

"Oh, Charlie," said Ellie, putting her arm around her friend. "Don't cry."

Just then, Jamila appeared.

"Hey, Charlie," Jamila said, concerned. "What's wrong? Are you ill?"

Charlie looked at her friend with tearful eyes and sniffed while Ellie explained what had happened.

"Well, it must be somewhere!" Jamila said brightly. "A bag can't just disappear, can it? It's not like we're part of some Harry Potter book. We've just got to find it."

Charlie said nothing and sniffed again.

"Jamila's right," said Ellie. "You must have put it somewhere else, not the place you thought you had."

"Don't worry, Charlie," said Jamila.

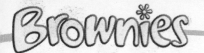

"We'll help you. We'll figure out where it is together."

"Thanks," Charlie replied weakly. "But will we find it in time for Brownies tonight?"

It wasn't until lunchtime that Jamila got the chance to tell Grace and Katie about the missing bag. Katie raced over to Charlie.

"How did you manage to lose it?" she wanted to know.

"She didn't do it on purpose!" Ellie pointed out.

"No, of course not," said Jamila.

"Sorry – I feel so stupid," sighed Charlie, looking tearful.

"We were supposed to take those things to Brownies tonight! This is an absolute disaster!" wailed Katie.

"I know…" Charlie sniffed.

"Come on," said Grace, putting her arm around her friend. "Katie didn't mean to be nasty, did you?" She looked at her sister expectantly.

Katie looked at Grace and then Charlie. "No – course not."

"I know we'll find it," said Grace. "We've just got to think back to what you were doing when you last saw the bag."

"Or when you last remember seeing it," Jamila suggested.

"Well," said Charlie, thinking. "Umm, after I got back home from Jamila's on Saturday I put the bag down by the front door, beneath where I hang my coat…"

"And then?" Katie pressed. "Did you put the bag in your bedroom?"

Charlie thought carefully. "No…"

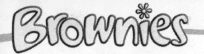

There was silence as the girls waited to hear what had happened.

"I was helping my mum with some jobs," said Charlie. "You know – like Vicky said Brownies should? I was lending a hand and helping to tidy up my sister Georgia's toys…"

"Then what did you do?" asked Jamila, quietly.

Charlie's eyes lit up.

"That's it!" she smiled. "I put Georgia's toys away in the toy box and then I put the bag of crafts in a safe place so that she wouldn't find them!"

"Great!" said Grace.

"So where's the safe place?" Katie wanted to know.

"My wardrobe!" Charlie declared.
"I thought I'd left them at the end of my bed,

only I didn't! 'Cos Georgia came into our
bedroom to read a story with me after her
bath – so I put the bag at the back of my
wardrobe!"

"Phew!" said Katie, and all the girls
giggled.

"I can't tell you how relieved I am –
thanks, you lot!" Charlie smiled.

As soon as she got home from school, Charlie looked in her wardrobe – and there was the bag stuffed full of Brownie crafts! She quickly changed into her Brownie outfit and then, after a quick snack with Boo, the two sisters set off to the Brownie hall with their mum and baby sister Georgia in her buggy.

Grace, Katie, Jamila and Ellie were already at the hall when Charlie and Boo arrived.

"Phew!" Jamila exclaimed. "Am I glad to see that bag!"

Chapter 8

Charlie presented the bag to Vicky and Sam as soon as she arrived at the hall.

"My goodness, you've been busy," said an amazed Sam. "How have you managed to make all these brilliant things?"

Vicky and Sam started to rummage through the goodies in the bag.

"Oh, it wasn't just me!" spluttered Charlie. She didn't want another misunderstanding!

"Who made them then?" Vicky asked.

"Grace and Katie, Ellie and Jamila, and me. We all made them over the last week." Charlie grinned. "And we've got some bits

83

and pieces we can use to make other things
and some gifts to sell as well."

"That's fantastic!" said Vicky. "Stickers for
all of you for all your hard work!"

"Great stuff, girls," agreed Sam. "Now – over to your Six tables to get ready for the Brownie Ring. We've got Eugenia coming again this evening!"

After the Brownies had settled into the Ring, and had sung their Brownie Welcome Song, Sam asked if anyone had any news to tell. Grace put up her hand.

"What would you like to say?" Sam asked.

"Well, I was wondering if you'd found that photo?" said Grace. "You know – the one of you and Vicky when you were Brownies?"

There was excited chatter from all the other Brownies as they remembered talking about it two weeks before. Vicky put up her right hand. Suddenly, everyone else did too and the hall fell silent again.

"Actually, we have brought one along!" Vicky smiled. She opened the folder on her

85

lap and brought out a large photo. She held it up. "Here we are!"

All the Brownies giggled.

"You're wearing woolly hats!" said Boo.

"And funny brown dresses!" added Holly.

"That's what we had to wear in those days," Sam laughed. "It made zooming around a bit more difficult than your skorts and leggings do! But we still had lots of Brownie fun."

"Oh!" said Vicky, looking at her watch. "I'll put the photo on the wall and you can all see it again later if you'd like to, but right now we need to get on or we'll run out of time. Eugenia will be here in a minute."

"Now," said Sam. "Hands up if you have been finishing off your Wildlife explorer badge."

Jamila, Charlie, Ellie, Katie and Grace were

among the Brownies who put up their hands.

"Perhaps you girls would like to come over to me while the others sing a song with Vicky," Sam continued. "Then I can check your work and see if everything is ready for you to get your badges!"

It was a short while later that, badge work and singing finished, the Brownies were called back in to the Brownie Ring. Eugenia had arrived and Vicky and Sam told the girls the details for the Craft Sale on Saturday. They had to turn up in their Brownie outfits, ready to help raise as much money as possible for the African medical centre. They were all told to bring as many shiny pennies as they could find for a Penny Race too!

"Well, it looks as if we've finished at just

the right time," said Sam, smiling at Eugenia who was carrying a large bag.

"Hello, Brownies!" said Eugenia, as Holly, Boo and Bethany rushed over to help her.

"Hello, Eugenia!" the Brownies all called back enthusiastically.

The Brownies hurried to help get a table ready for her in the middle of the hall. Then Eugenia started to take things out of her mysterious bag.

"What have you got there?" Bethany asked.

"Some African fruit and vegetables," Eugenia explained. "These come from all over the African region, not just Senegal and South Africa. I thought you might like to try some of them."

The Brownies excitedly helped Eugenia put the fruit and vegetables on plates on the table.

"We've got mangoes, bananas, papayas, ginger, guavas, passion fruit, coconuts and okra," said Eugenia. "Then I've also brought some green beans and sugar snap peas – those *are* grown in Senegal. Who wants to have a guess at which one is which?"

Eugenia had written out some labels with the names of the fruit and vegetables on them. The Brownies giggled as they tried to work out where each label belonged.

"This is definitely a coconut!" declared Boo. "I know because I've seen them at the funfair."

All the Brownies recognized the bananas and they also knew the peas and beans. But when it came to the other things, Eugenia had to help them out. The fruit looked so delicious that there was no shortage of volunteers to taste it.

"Would Brownies in Africa eat these things all the time?" Ashvini asked.

"Well, I don't know about all the time," Eugenia replied. "Not all of them would be available in every African country – and they wouldn't be grown all year round, either.

But lots of African Brownies and Guides would know exactly what they were."

"Cool!" Charlie said.

"Now," said Vicky. "I think it's time to tidy away the left over fruit and vegetables and get on with some dancing!"

"Dancing?" said Grace excitedly. She loved dancing and went to a ballet class every week. "What kind of dancing?"

"African dancing!" Sam said. "Come on – let's clear the table away and get started."

Soon, all the Brownies were watching Eugenia as she showed them the steps to a South African dance. She explained that the different countries in Africa all had their own dances. Then she got out a CD player, put on some African music and stood in front of the girls. As the beat of the music filled the hall, Eugenia and the Brownies found it

impossible not to sway along with it.

"OK." Eugenia smiled, moving her feet to the rhythm. "Let's go!"

All round the hall, everyone was soon dancing to the catchy music.

"This is brilliant!" Jamila said to Grace, who was dancing next to her.

"It's really good fun!" Grace agreed, "and so different from ballet!"

"Well done, Brownies!" Eugenia grinned. "You've got it!"

When the music stopped, the Brownies took a breather.

"Now," she said. "Are there any musicians here?"

Poppy – one of the Hedgehogs, Jamila, Molly from the Rabbits, and Chloe and Jasmine from the Badgers all put up their hands.

"Excellent!" said Eugenia. "Good job I've brought some drums and shakers with me then. Who wants which one?"

The drums were small ones that you could hold in the crook of your arm. The shakers were made from brightly-coloured plastic, and were filled with lots of tiny beans.

"Right," said Eugenia. "You choose if you want to dance or play! Let's have the musicians over here…" she pointed to her right. "And the dancers over here…" she pointed to her left. "Let's get playing and dancing!"

Half an hour later, the 1st Badenbridge Brownies had mastered an African dance and music routine.

"I can't believe how fantastic you all are!" Eugenia said, giving them a clap. "I can't wait to see you do that on Saturday!"

"Saturday?" the Brownies wondered.

"Yes," said Sam. "We thought you could sing and dance on Saturday to get everyone's attention in the High Street."

"Wow! How cool is that?" Ellie exclaimed.

"Totally cool!" replied Jamila.

"Right, everyone," said Vicky, "let's get into our Brownie Ring. It's already time to finish and I can see people arriving to take you home."

Quickly, the Brownies gathered to say their goodbyes, and Vicky and Sam handed each of them a sheet with all the information they needed for the Craft Sale.

"See you all on Saturday, outside the supermarket," Vicky said.

"And don't be late!" warned Sam.

"That was a brilliant meeting!" said an excited Katie to the others as they waited to be collected.

"It was! But then Brownies is always brilliant," said Grace.

"Yes and we've got the Craft Sale and Thinking Day on Saturday," said Ellie.

"And Sam has said that we'll all get our Wildlife explorer badges at the next Brownie meeting," said Charlie.

"Our first ever Brownie badges!" exclaimed Jamila.

"Yesss!" the best friends all said at once.

Chapter 9

The sale was due to start at 1.30p.m. Vicky and Sam had told the Brownies to be outside the supermarket a bit early so they could get everything ready. They'd already put up two tables with Daisy's help outside the shop's window by the time the first Brownies began to arrive. Now all they had to do was decorate the tables and unpack their crafts.

"Right," Sam said, glancing round at the Brownies, who looked smart in their Brownie outfits and were ready for action. "First of all, we need to put these tablecloths on the tables."

"I'll help," said Jamila, Katie, Charlie and Ellie all at once. They looked at each other and giggled.

"Two of you do the one table, and two of you do the other one," Sam suggested. "Then we'll need to put all your gorgeous crafts out on display. But before that, I'd better check that everyone's here."

As Jamila and Katie unfolded their tablecloth, Ellie and Charlie grabbed the other one, Grace helped Vicky carry the bags of sale goodies over to the tables, and Sam ticked names off her list.

"Right – we're just waiting for Sukia," Sam said. "And Eugenia said she would be along later. Sukia is bringing some leaflets about HealthHelp so that we can tell people about who we are raising money for."

Vicky went over to help the girls putting

out the tablecloths. They were ones that the 1st Badenbridge Brownies always used for important events. They were in the Brownie colours of brown and yellow and had "1st Badenbridge Brownies" written in big writing across the edge that hung down along the sides of the table. On either side of the writing was the Brownie Trefoil emblem. The girls thought they looked great.

1st Badenbridge Brownies

The Brownies spent ages deciding how best
to arrange their crafts on the tables. In the end,
they decided to put the jewellery they had
made from the beads on one side of the first
table, and friendship bracelets in all the colours
of the rainbow on the other side. Then they
arranged cards and gift tags, made from
recycled Christmas and birthday cards, in
bundles on the second table. Finally, other gifts
like the frog beanbags, bottles of bubble bath,
decorated picture frames and painted pots
were put in the remaining space.

"Wow!" said Charlie, stepping back on the
pavement to take a look at the result of the
Brownies' hard work. "That looks amazing!"

"Now," said Vicky. "We've also got our
banner to put up. Daisy and I made it last
night. Can you girls help me, please? The
supermarket has given us permission to put

it up against this window."

Chloe, Jamila, Molly, Boo and Charlie held the banner. In gigantic letters it said:

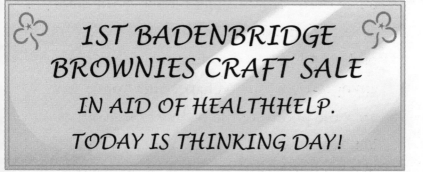

1ST BADENBRIDGE BROWNIES CRAFT SALE
IN AID OF HEALTHHELP.
TODAY IS THINKING DAY!

"I don't think anyone will be able to pass by without noticing us," declared Sam.

"It's brill, Daisy – well done!" Ellie said enthusiastically.

"Hey!" said Katie. "Here's Sukia. She's with her mum – and a gigantic poster!"

"Hello, Sukia! Hello, Aletha!" Sam and Vicky smiled. "My goodness – what do you have there?"

"It's a poster about Auntie's health centre," Sukia explained. "Mum and I made it last night. It's got lots of information about the charity and Auntie sent us some photos of the people who work at the centre with her, so we added them to the display too. We've also made some leaflets all about HealthHelp to hand out to people."

All the Brownies gathered round to look at Sukia and her mum's hard work.

"This is really good," said Jamila.

"It tells you everything about the health centre," agreed Charlie. "It's perfect."

As the Brownies admired the display, some people came out of the supermarket and walked over to the Brownie tables.

"Come on!" said Vicky. "Let's put this noticeboard up so that people can see it! It looks like we've got our first customers already!"

The 1st Badenbridge Brownies' Craft Sale got off to a flying start. The Brownies took it in turns to stand behind the tables and sell the goodies they had made. When they weren't selling things, they were shaking donation buckets, decorated with the Brownie Trefoil, that Sam had brought along.

"Shake those buckets, girls," Sam encouraged them. "You never know, people might have some loose change to put in. The more we raise the better!"

"And if we get enough coins, we could use them in our Penny Race to make a

Trefoil as well," suggested Vicky. "We did that for Thinking Day last year."

"Cool!" said the Brownies.

"Look," said Charlie. "Here's Eugenia!"

"Hello, Brownies!" Eugenia grinned. "My goodness, doesn't this all look fantastic!"

"It's great, isn't it?" agreed Jamila.

"And the health centre display is such a good idea," Eugenia said.

"Are we going to dance soon?" Grace asked.

"You bet!" declared Eugenia. "Let me just get my things sorted out. Then we can get out our drums, put on our dancing shoes, and get moving to that African rhythm!"

With the sound of the music, the beat of the drum, and the rhythm of the dancing, the 1st Badenbridge Brownies stopped the people on the High Street in their tracks.

When they finished their dance with a big, joyous shout at the end, the audience cheered and clapped.

Jamila, Charlie, Grace, Katie and Ellie looked at each other and grinned from ear to ear. They hadn't had this much fun in ages. Nor, from the looks on their faces, had the other Brownies.

"Isn't this brilliant?" Charlie said.

Jamila nodded.

"And it looks like we're raising lots of money too," said Katie.

"Yes," added Grace. "The leaflets about the health centre have almost run out!"

"Hey!" Ellie asked, pointing to a tall man holding a camera. He was talking to Vicky and Sam. "Wasn't that the man who came to see us when we went to the Nature Centre a few weeks ago?"

"Yes! He's the man from the Badenbridge Reporter!" exclaimed Charlie. "He was taking photographs of us when we were playing and dancing."

Vicky raised her right hand and turned round, looking at the Brownies. Immediately, they also raised their right hands and fell silent.

"Well done, Brownies!" Vicky grinned. "I expect you'll remember Steven Hunt from the local paper? He wants to take another photo for next week's paper. So can we all gather round, please?"

"Yeah!" cried all the Brownies, quickly getting into position.

"Say 'BROWNIES'!" Steven smiled as he took the picture.

"Come on then, Brownies," said Sam when the photo was done. "Time for our

Penny Race. Let's see if we have enough pennies to make a Thinking Day Trefoil!"

"How do we do that?" Jamila asked.

"Well, first of all Daisy draws a chalk picture of the Trefoil on the pavement," said Sam. "We get Daisy to do it because she's better at drawing than me and Vicky!"

The Brownies giggled and watched as Daisy started drawing. She was doing a really great job.

"Won't we get in trouble for drawing on the pavement though?" Grace worried.

"It's OK," said Vicky. "The chalk will wipe off easily when we're done."

"OK," said Daisy, standing up and looking at the Trefoil she'd drawn. "Who's remembered their race pennies?"

"Me!" said all of the 1st Badenbridge Brownies at the same time.

Vicky and Sam laughed.

"Well, one at a time, place your pennies on our Trefoil," said Vicky.

"Yes," agreed Sam. "Let's see if we can complete the whole Trefoil in shiny Thinking Day Pennies!"

One by one, the Brownies laid their pennies on the pattern Daisy had drawn. Very soon, the Trefoil was finished and shining on the pavement.

"That looks great!" said Ellie.

"Sure does!" agreed Grace, taking a photo of it with her camera.

"Fantastic, Brownies!" said Vicky. "Let's give ourselves a big World Thinking Day clap!"

With everything sold and the tables empty of goodies, Vicky and Sam declared the 1st Badenbridge Brownies' Thinking Day Craft Sale over later that afternoon. The girls all helped to pack away the tablecloths and noticeboard.

"That was an excellent day, Brownies," Sam grinned.

"Yes – well done, everyone!" Vicky said. "You should all be very proud of yourselves. Now, if your parents are here, then you have permission to go home. See you all next week, when we'll discover how much money we've raised!"

The Brownies could barely wait!

Chapter 10

On Monday, after school, the girls were hanging out in Jamila's room.

"Saturday was great," sighed Charlie.

"It was really good to be part of our first outing as proper Brownies, wasn't it?" Jamila agreed.

"Yeah! Plus we sold all our arts and crafts," said Ellie.

"Do you think we raised much money?" Grace wondered.

"It looked like there was loads in the donation buckets," said Katie, "and lots of money for our Trefoil of Thinking Day Pennies too, so we should have."

"I can't wait to find out tomorrow!" said Charlie. "And to get our badges too!"

"Come on," grinned Jamila. "Let's go and get some tea!"

When the five friends arrived at the hall for Brownies the following night, there was already a buzz of excitement.

"The District Commissioner is here!" Daisy told them as soon as they came in. "And Eugenia has come back too!"

"Who's the District Commissioner?" Katie asked.

"She looks after Rainbows, Brownies and Guides in all the units and groups in our district," Daisy explained.

"Sounds like she's really important," said Charlie.

"Sounds like she's really scary!" said Ellie.

"She's not scary!" Daisy laughed. "She's really nice. But she is important because she looks after so many of us."

"So why has she come to be with our Brownie unit tonight?" Jamila wondered.

"Because of the Craft Sale," said Daisy. "She's come to find out how we did."

But before the girls could ask Daisy any more questions, Sam raised her right hand and the Brownies all fell silent.

"Time for a Brownie Ring!" she called.

With the District Commissioner in the hall, every Brownie raced to their places in the Brownie Ring. Fortunately, not a single Brownie had forgotten any part of her Brownie outfit or Promise Box.

"I'm impressed," the District Commissioner said, smiling at the Brownies. "Now I hear that you had a terrific day on Saturday. Who would like to tell me what you were doing?"

Boo's hand shot up.

"We were raising money for Sukia's auntie's charity in Senegal," Boo explained.

"Excellent," the District Commissioner said. "And why did you decide to do that?"

"Because we found out about her auntie's charity when we were talking about being a Brownie in Africa," said Bethany.

"So what made you talk about the Brownies in Africa?" the District Commissioner wondered.

115

"Oh!" said Katie, her arm waving in a sea of other Brownie arms.

The District Commissioner pointed at her. "Why don't you tell me?"

"Because we were talking about Thinking Day," Katie explained. "And we decided that some Brownies and their friends might need some help from Brownies here."

"Very good." the District Commissioner smiled. "And what did you find out about the Brownies in the African region?"

Even more Brownies put up their hands. They took it in turns to tell the District Commissioner all that they had learned about the food the Brownies in African countries might eat, and the clothes the Brownies might wear – all the things the girls had been finding out about since they first decided what to do for Thinking Day.

"Would you like to see our African dance?"
Eugenia asked the District Commissioner.

She smiled. "Yes, please!"

Eugenia grinned. "Come on then,
Brownies – let's dance!"

A while later, after the Brownies had also
taught the District Commissioner how to do
the dance and beat the rhythm on the drums
and shakers, the tired and happy 1st
Badenbridge Brownies gathered in their
Brownie Ring. It was already getting near
the end of their meeting.

"Now," said Sam, "you've all worked very
hard. And the really excellent
news is that we've raised two
hundred pounds for
HealthHelp in Senegal!"

HealthHelp
Two Hundred Pounds Only   £200.00

"Yeah!" cheered the Brownies.

The five friends looked at each other and grinned.

"Well done," Sam laughed. "Now as part of preparing for the Craft Sale, most of you have been working towards the Craft badge."

"Yes," said the District Commissioner. "I saw some photos of the beautiful things you made. And I understand that some of you have just completed your Wildlife explorer badge as well. You are busy Brownies! So I would like the following girls to come over and collect both their badges, please!"

The District Commissioner called out a long list of names and Charlie, Jamila, Grace, Katie and Ellie's names were on it!

"Our first two Brownie badges!" Katie squealed.

"And we're being presented with them by the District Commissioner!" Jamila smiled.

"This is just the best!" said Grace.

As the last of the Brownies were awarded their badges, they all settled down again ready for Vicky and Sam to end the evening.

"Now, before we sing 'Brownie Bells'," said Vicky, "some of you will remember Lottie's idea for a Thinking Day cake. Well Daisy has kindly helped Lottie to make everyone a little cake to take home with them! They've each got a name of a country where there are Brownies iced on top of them."

"Yeah!" the Brownies all cheered again.

Vicky put up her right hand. The hall fell silent.

"Now, before we really do have to go home, I'd like to ask Jessica, our Foxes Sixer, to read a Thought for Thinking Day."

Jessica took the special book in which the Brownies wrote down their Thoughts for the

Week from underneath her yellow Promise
Box.

"We think about all our Brownie friends
around the world," Jessica said. "We think
about what we did for Thinking Day and our
Craft Sale. We hope we can help Brownies
and other children in Africa with the money
we raised. We think about Vicky and Sam
who run Brownies and do loads of fun things
with us," she added. "Oh – and we think
about the District Commissioner who helps
us too!"

"We do!" agreed all the other Brownies.

After singing "Brownie Bells", Vicky
looked at the Brownies and asked, "What do
Brownies do every day?"

"A good turn!" they all shouted.

"And what's the best thing in the world?"
Sam asked.

"BROWNIES!" they all screamed back.
Because they all knew it was.

How Ellie got her Craft badge!

1. She made African beads. Eugenia showed Ellie and the other Brownies how to mould the beads, and the girls painted them bright colours and made necklaces and bracelets out of them when they were dry.

2. She learned how to make friendship bracelets. Vicky and Sam taught the Brownies to weave and plait brightly-coloured threads together to make fun jewellery.

3. She decorated a mirror using glass paints. Using the Brownie flower as inspiration, Ellie created a gorgeous design for her mirror!

Craft

GLUE

Make Your Own African Beads!

You will need:

Kitchen roll
A mug
A large mixing bowl
Metal spoon
Sieve
3 tablespoons plain flour
4 tablespoons water
Plastic drinking straws
A plate
Paints and brush
Wool

1. Tear the kitchen roll into small pieces to fill about four mugs. Place it in the mixing bowl and cover with warm water. Soak for a few minutes.

2. Mix the wet paper to a pulp and then squeeze the water out through the sieve. Leave the pulp in the sieve.

3. In the mixing bowl, mix the flour and water into a gluey paste. Add the paper and mix well.

4. Press a blob of the paper pulp around a straw to make a bead shape.

5. Make lots of beads in different shapes and sizes.

6. When the beads are partly dry, take them off the straw and leave to dry on a plate.

7. When the beads are completely dry, paint them. Try painting some of them with dots, stripes or other patterns. Leave the beads to dry.

8. Now thread the beads on to wool to make necklaces and bracelets!

Activity instructions taken from *Brownies Adventure On*, published by Girlguiding UK.

Collect the other books in the series!

And look out for...

Brownies
Christmas cheer

Caroline Plais...

Christmas is coming, and the 1st Badenbridge Brownies are getting in to the spirit of things! With crafts to make for the local Christmas market, festive goodies to bake for the unit party, and a trip to the local pantomime to look forward to, the girls eagerly set about spreading Christmas cheer. Now, if only it would snow…

Join the Brownies

Brownies do it all!

They do cool things to get badges like the Artist badge and the Computer badge, they have sleepovers, they make heaps of friends and have lots of fun.

Brownies are aged from seven to ten and are part of Girlguiding UK, the largest organization for girls and young women in the UK, which has around 575,000 members.

To learn more about what Brownies get up to, visit www.girlguiding.org.uk/brownies or call 0800 169 5901 to find out how you can join in the fun.